The Trip

TO MARSHA ROTH

EZRA JACK KEATS
The Trip

ISBN 0-590-05419-8

12 11 10 9 8 7 6 5 4   8 9/8 0 1 2 3/9

Printed in the U.S.A.   08

SCHOLASTIC INC.

Louie's family moved to a new neighborhood.
He didn't know anybody there.
No kids, no dogs, no cats.
And there weren't even any steps
in front of the door to sit on.
Louie sighed and went in.

He got an old shoebox.
He made a hole in the front,
cut out the back and part of the top,
and began to paste things inside.

He taped a piece of colored plastic on the top
of the box, and another piece on the end.
He hung his plane from the top, and closed the box.

Louie looked through the hole.

WOW!

Louie pretended he was flying his plane.
He flew higher and higher—over the moon.

He landed in his old
neighborhood.
It was very quiet.

He wandered around.
He could hear
his own footsteps.
Where was everybody?

He passed Roberto's old house—
and stopped suddenly.

He turned around
and ran—as fast
as he could.

He was trapped!

"Hey, wait—I know that tail!
It's the cat! And you're Roberto,
and that must be Amy and Archie."

They were his old friends!
"Surprise!" they yelled.
"Trick or treat!"

Louie took them for a ride
on his plane.
Everybody ran to the windows
to look at them.

It was time to go home.

Everyone was waving.

"Trick or treat!" Louie heard from far away.

"Come on, Louie," his mother was saying.
"Let me help you on with your costume."
They could hear the kids outside yelling,
"Trick or treat, trick or treat!"

Louie went outside
to join them.

Here's how you can make a peep show like Louie's.

1.
Get an old shoebox
and make a hole
in the front.

2.
Cut out the back
and make a window
in the top of the box.

3.
Tape cut-outs of buildings
inside the box.

4.
Hang a paper plane on
a string from the top.

5.
Tape a piece of
clear colored plastic
over the window on the top.
Tape another piece
over the back.

Now you are ready to watch the show.